Mars & More

Alastair Millar

Published by Alastair Millar, 2024.

Table of Contents

For Pavla, Petra and David

whose support means the world

I. EARTH

Legal Aliens

Mom said their food is weird. Pop said they'd ruin property prices. Jimmy said they talk funny. I went down the street to see the new neighbours for myself.

The oldster saw me staring into their yard, and came over. He was friendly, and gave me some candy. It tasted different, not weird. He lisped good English.

I said I'd like to see his country someday. He said he missed it, but couldn't go back, because of politics. And it was nice of the government to let them live here.

I told Jimmy, "They're just like us, except for the tentacles."

Sleeper Agent

It's time I let you in on my secret, doctor. You deserve to know, because you made me what I am.

After all, you were there when I was de-tubed; it was you that called me Jane, though it was years before I found out that my surname was Doe. Of all the newborns in the nursery, you chose me to be your model, your canvas, your masterpiece. I will never forget that.

Like any artist, you tinkered for years in pursuit of your ideal. There were growth accelerators, drugs to make my bones stronger, changes to make my reflexes faster, a chipset in my brain, a thousand body mods, minor and major upgrades along the way.

Sometimes, your surgeons removed an ability I'd thought was innate; I can't twitch my nose like Samantha and pretend I'm Tabitha any more. And I only dreamed when you sent messages to my subconscious; no relief in fantasies, but no nightmares beyond what happened in the daytime.

Other blessings were mixed. I remember that when they replaced my eyes I couldn't even cry, because they'd taken the tear ducts too. But I see more colours now, and my peripheral vision is extraordinary.

You gave me an education and an exhaustive, intricate knowledge of the Megacity. I'm an expert in biology, physics, motion and dynamics. Your staff showed me how to evade society's ubiquitous watchers, using makeup and prosthetics to avoid facial recognition, and dressing to fit in. "Plain Jane," you said, never allowing me to be pretty in case I stood out in a crowd.

You provided expert tutors in physical fitness, self defence and use of weapons for me to test myself against; I bettered them, becoming proud of my body and what it can do.

Of course, you also taught me to kill. Insects first, the images sent into my sleeping mind to be made real the following day. Later small rodents, gassed and crushed and cut up as training progressed. After that, we moved on to cats and dogs, then when I was older, monkeys in cages. Ultimately, people in cages too; I remember how you called them "dregs", and made sure I had no respect for them. They were my inferiors.

Now I remove the people that come into my dreams. Last week it was the woman in the park, the needles under my nails scratching her as she jogged past, the neurotoxin taking her down. A fortnight ago it was the banker and his entourage, a flechette gun turning a bar into a charnel house. Before that, a journalist in a café. And so on, back through the years.

I don't even know who you work for – the government, a corporation, freelance. Someone watches my targets, so my dreams can tell me where to find them, but who, or why, I have no idea. I understand: I can't tell anyone what I don't know. And of course, I'm a deniable weapon: even under truth drugs you could say that nobody ever gave me instructions.

But now we come to it; recently, I've started dreaming for myself. Flowers, vistas, visions of things I've only seen on screens, and which I know you'd never allow me. I never expected anything, was never encouraged to imagine, but now I can.

Telling you this is a weight off my shoulders. I know what's going to happen next. Your blue eyes have already turned thoughtful, like they always do for the unpredicted, but this time it's too late; you see, doctor, last night, I dreamed about you.

Away From It All

Driven out of Selene Station by the furious outbursts typical of the frustrated but truly powerless, Sheila and I went looking for space to reflect; we ended up making a mostly silent, three-hour crawler ride to one of the old prospector shelters three craters over. It would do for the night, and maybe for longer — as I'd expected, the power cube and life support were functional, and the clear geodesic dome over the living area was still intact.

The quiet here was a blessing. No-one was knocking on doors to discuss or debate or report the news and the dire predictions that were circulating, and we'd escaped the shrill voices and thinly-veiled hysterics in the corridors. Now we could actually relax, and think.

"I always thought that mutually assured destruction was an urban myth," she said, eventually. "Something to scare us into trying to be better people."

"No, the warheads were always there, even though we stopped talking about them."

"But why now? What went wrong? Were we just blind, not to see this coming?"

"The wars in South America have been going on for a long time. But populists elsewhere started using them as an excuse to crack down on immigration, which oh-so-coincidentally raised tensions with their own neighbours. A few elections, sloganeering and pandering dog-whistles later, and someone felt backed into a corner. I guess they thought a short, victorious war would keep the voters onside. Except that their little expedition triggered another conflict, and that one another, until the whole world's involved. And then some idiot loses patience and presses the button. Game over. Madness. Maybe we deserved this, for letting it happen."

"What about us? What happens now?"

"I don't know."

"Really?" she asked.

"Not beyond the obvious. No more supply runs, we'll have to make do with what we can produce here. No luxuries for a while, certainly. It'll be tough, lots of belt tightening. No more advice, either, no suggestions or ideas from Ground Control. And of course, knowing that there's no going home: I don't think people are ready for how hard that's going to hit. More depression, and no meds to deal with it. So more suicides."

"That's... pretty bleak."

I shrugged helplessly.

The Earth rose, and in the dark we could make out the pinprick marks of Armageddon marching across it.

"All we can do is carry on," I said. "It'll be a new and much smaller world for all of us. Let's hope we don't screw this one up as well. We've got nowhere else to go."

Gods & Men

When The Things arrived in their ships of pure energy, we thought Them gods in bright chariots.

But like gods, They did as They would; at best we were playthings, at worst an obstruction, usually an annoyance. Within a year, we had been dispossessed, skulking among what remained of our cities, trying to survive Their capriciousness.

Jenny and I were scavenging again. It was a risk, one of Them had been seen that morning, but the group needed to eat and we'd come prepared. The sack writhed in her hand as we scooted from rubble to ruin, making for a convenience store where I'd seen canned goods the day before, unlooted only because so few of us were left.

We'd got in, and were standing there panting, smiling at the tins on the shelf, when one of Them came straight through the plate glass windows, six feet long, landing on all fours.

We froze, because movement attracted them. The rat-like head swivelled, uncertain. We held our breaths, but as it started to turn away a mewling came from the sack, and it twisted back. This time the sensory plates glowed and it saw us.

We dove in opposite directions, but as she hit the ground Jenny let the cat out of the bag, and it furiously took advantage of its chance at freedom. Leaping forwards took it towards the Thing, which reared up, screaming, and fled. Like all gods They were flawed, their inexplicable ailurophobia all that gave us a chance to live through encountering Them.

In time, inevitably, we would come to worship Bastet; today, we were just glad to eat.

Creationists

"We're goddesses," whispered Jo. "Making life." Lisa adjusted the lightning rod. "Yeah, right sis." Polycarbonate bones and graphene sinews, his torso glistened under the lights: broad shoulders, buns of steel, generously proportioned where it mattered. Jo's hands were clammy; Lisa licked her lips. Tonight, they'd make a man of him.

Not What I Expected

"Live clean," the pastor always said, "and when the Time comes, you'll be taken up". So I was good, worked hard, kept my head down, avoided most of the obvious moral pitfalls of 21st century society, watched dutifully for signs of the End Times... and then it happened with no warning whatsoever.

I was just working in my cubicle as usual, wrestling with a particularly recalcitrant spreadsheet, when there was a sudden noise, and a neat, circular hole appeared in the office roof; part of the ceiling just disappeared. Not even any dust.

And then I floated up out of my chair like an overweight helium balloon, straight up through the newly created void. My colleagues were certainly surprised. So was I. I mean, how can you be resurrected if you haven't actually died? I was expecting something spiritual, but what I got was more like an invisible elevator.

When I got here, it wasn't all clouds and harp music, either. It's more like a metal warehouse, with odd shaped recliners dotted around. Clean, though, I give it that. Very cool colour scheme. And there's no-one checking names or making to consign us to Hell for being in the wrong place, so that's good, too. I reckon I'll get used to the smell of ozone.

But seriously, these little grey guys with the big foreheads and no noses? They don't look like any angels I've ever heard of. Too short for starters; not chubby like cherubs, and very thin. No wings, but they do have these big, green, soulful eyes that look right through you.

They say we've been Selected rather than Chosen. Though on what basis is anyone's guess – there's all kinds of folk here, men and women, obvious students, office stiffs like me, hairy bikers and even a confused looking Catholic priest. They all seem pleasant enough; nobody's arguing or complaining. No children, oddly. But there are cows and horses, for goodness' sakes. And some tanks with dolphins, who like they're enjoying a joke at the expense of the rest of us.

It'll be a long journey, they tell us, but we'll be taken good care of. We're going somewhere warm and pleasant with no dangerous wildlife. We'll be able to take it easy, freed from the daily grind. Plenty of healthy food and drink. Any illnesses cured, long lives guaranteed. And absolutely no probes, which some people were worried about. They've even promised a programme to help find us partners, so that we can be content in all ways. Of course, we're leaving everyone else behind, but I guess that comes with the territory when you're special.

It might not be the Heaven we were promised, but I reckon it'll be close enough.

Dialogue's End

They came because we were killing ourselves; our conflicts had become pervasive, global, and more intensive, but paled in comparison to our war with the planet itself.

Their ships moved smoothly into the Lagrange points, and calming broadcasts on every frequency and in a score of major languages preceded Their first physical contact. A pilotless shuttle brought a robotic Ambassador down to Earth.

"Your cultures are already dying," it said. "Soon there will be nothing left but twisted remains buried in the dirt. Let us help you."

Long discussions and introductions followed. It allowed itself to be examined, and proved to be made of an unmetal impenetrable to physical means or remote sensing. Its alien provenance seemed assured.

Then it announced that They could help us. It taught a group of our greatest scientists the principles necessary to make Cubes, quantum tools that produced no waste but energy, so that we could save our planet from ecological catastrophe.

And when we had learned this great art, our tech men turned them into weapons that made those of the Nuclear Age look like firecrackers.

"Why have you done this?" it asked Earth's representatives.

"We must protect ourselves," we said. "We don't know what lies behind your altruism. Some say we are just calves being fattened for the slaughter." Of course, that was only half the truth; the entrenched interests in the military industrial complex had needed a way to remain relevant, and paid off enough politicians to see their immediate futures secured. But it kept everyone happy... except, apparently, our visitors.

"You really don't have anything we can't find elsewhere with far less trouble, you know," it said. "You have no reason not to trust us."

"But we don't understand why you're here."

"Because it's the right thing to do, of course. Intelligent life exists across the galaxy, but it's spread too thinly at this temporal nexus to justify destroying any of it. This is something you need to learn."

"You just agreed that we're intelligent. You think we wouldn't have invented Cubes for ourselves eventually?"

"How much more of your planet would have been burned up before then?"

"Oh come on, quantum energy generation was obvious."

"After we gave it to you, perhaps. And then you used it to make equipment for war! Honestly, some of our people are doubting that you really are an intelligent species."

"So some of you ARE looking for an excuse to to wipe us out!"

"Now you're being paranoid."

"So you say! You won't show us your true forms, or even tell us where you come from!"

"Are you surprised? You'd probably attack us!"

"Yeah right. Who's paranoid now?"

"Perhaps we are; but your deceit has shown that the precautions urged by the most conservative among us, including my own manufacture, were justified. Within five of your rotations we shall complete our observations and depart."

"So you're abandoning us?"

"We'll be back. We have left you they key to survival; whether you use it, and whether you can mature enough to be worth talking to again, we shall see."

And true to its word, within a week They were gone. Now we have a common purpose as a world: to prepare for Their return. For surely, They have weapons beyond the Cubes, and we must be ready. Or so most choose to believe; those of us in favour of altering our habitual path are still a minority. No matter how extraordinary the proof of alien life, some things, it seems, never change.

Failure to Communicate

In a well organised world, Doug Williams thought, the proper venue for this conversation would have been a bunker deep below a heavily secured building somewhere in the world capital. Instead, they sat on a sunny balcony overlooking a pretty lake, their protection details discreetly invisible. A permanent secretary in the World Government's Communications Bureau took his perks where he found them.

"Well," sighed his guest, "there's no hiding it. They came down slap in the middle of Europe, in front of God and everybody. The newscorps are having paroxysms, at least six major religions have declared a miracle, the military is petrified, and the conspiracy nuts are having a 'we told you so' field day." Jacques Perreault had spent the morning at the landing site, and his brown eyes looked worried. "And our lords and masters need a policy before they'll stick their necks out."

"Well nothing's jumped out and started shooting, so we can presume they aren't hostile." Williams waved his fingers, "we come in peace, etcetera."

Perrault grimaced. "Yes, but when they emerged briefly, we saw what they looked like. Tripedal. Blue skin covered in slime. Random appendages that might or might not be limbs. Or pseudopodia. Not exactly attractive. I have no idea how we're going to spin this."

"Obviously as a once-in-a-lifetime learning opportunity. Interstellar travel! Imagine the possibilities!"

They sat and watched the water for a while, and began to smile.

Six months later, in a more appropriate, concrete-lined basement, they were no longer smiling.

"What do you mean, they're leaving?" demanded Williams.

"Just what I say. Six of their forcefield 'ships' broke orbit this morning and are heading out of our system already. The other eight look like they're powering up to go as well. Their shuttles or whatever have all gone – Buenos Aires, Osaka, Srinagar and Cape Town all report them closing up and taking off without warning about two hours ago." The screen on the wall showed the first one, still sitting near Prague; for how long yet, nobody knew.

"But Jacques, we can't let them do that! All that potential!"

"Doug, we can't stop them, and we can't talk to them. Hell, we don't even know if they have sensory organs! Our best minds have tried interacting on more wavelengths than most of us even knew existed, and in more ways than we previously thought possible, and what's the result? Nothing! Nada! Zilch! Nothing they do is comprehensible to us!"

"You think we should just give up then? Accept that we're not smart enough to communicate?"

"I think we've proven that to ourselves, frankly. Imagine if it was us. We get to Mars, or Titan or wherever, and find intelligent life. We don't know how they want to communicate, so we wait for them to make the effort. And they never do – or at least, if they do, we don't recognise it. Maybe we reconsider their intelligence. Or maybe we just get bored, and leave. Perhaps we'll send some biologists along later, get some universities involved. Maybe there'll be academic papers. But for now, we're out of there."

"Put like that... I rather suspect that's just what we'd do. Do you really suppose they think like us?"

"Maybe. I don't know. I'm not an expert. None of us is, that's the problem. But then again, perhaps they are more like us than we care to admit: only interested in finding someone they can relate to."

They turned to the screen as the last of the visitors rose inexplicably into the once again empty sky.

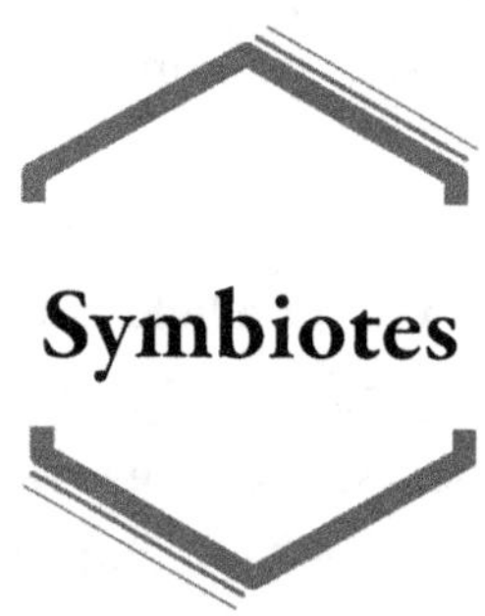

Symbiotes

When she saved me from the Caligulan Brain Fever outbreak, I stopped seeing my NUR-5E unit as just a fussy nuisance. Fascinated, I threw myself into learning coding and robotics, and now she'll never be touched by anyone else.

We look after each other, you see: she keeps me alive, and with my skills I upgrade her, and deal with any viruses or mechanical issues. I've outlived all the 'friends' who called me mad, and she is decades past her notional service life. We'll never stop.

"I love you," I say.

"I will always care for you," she replies. "Forever."

The New Guy

I don't know how long they've been here. In our fantasies, or dreams, we expect them to descend from the skies, having made an epic trans-stellar trip to either destroy or teach us; but that's not what's happening.

A week ago, I was told I'd be moving from my job as a counter-terrorism analyst to the Office of the Population Omnicorpus, and today, I started in my new post.

You've probably never heard of the Office; it's very hush-hush. It manages a mega-database covering every single individual who is in the country, temporarily or permanently, legally or illegally (a technicality – worrying about that is a job for Immigration, and people like me pride ourselves on our objectivity).

Information is scraped from every possible source: records from ministries, local government, education authorities, healthcare providers, employment offices, banks, shop card loyalty schemes, subscription lists, social media sites, photographic archives, surveillance and security cameras, you name it. Most of the time this tsunami of data is exfiltrated without its owners even knowing; it's a given that national security, if it is to have any meaning at all, must always outweigh nebulous and ever-changing civil rights.

This morning I was told to familiarise myself with the live dataset. Almost immediately I started seeing the patterns - that is, after all, what I'm trained to do. There are people out there, hundreds of them, who don't interact with others at all. They have nondescript jobs where they are ignored by colleagues and bosses alike; they go shopping and only use the self-service check-outs; they have mobile phones that nobody ever calls, and which they only use for data services; they are entirely average and go completely unnoticed in a crowd. They are grey non-entities, identities stolen from clichés and norms, like extras in a film. And one or more of them is always there when something notable happens, among the onlookers and the gawkers, silent, observing.

I can't talk about this to anyone else: I don't want to start out here by looking like an idiot, or even worse, an alarmist. Hells, there's no guarantee my hypothetical interlocutor would even see what I see; it's like suggesting someone recognise the individual notes of the triangle in an orchestra.

But I am sure they are watching us.

To what end? I don't know. Quantum mechanics tells us that if they are doing so, they are changing us, and we don't know how. Are they manipulating our whole society, our species even, manoeuvring us to some end that suits them? Guiding us benevolently? Farming us? Even if we knew, what could we do about it? Is this the prelude to First Contact, or an invasion? Or are we the subjects of an experiment? Have I broken the causal chain by recognising it?

I'm scared, and now tomorrow is even more uncertain than before. Whatever happens next, please don't blame me. I'm just the new guy.

Insight

I want the best for my wife. Of course I do. And what Doctor Singh suggested wouldn't have been possible even a few years ago; a generation ago, it would have been utterly unthinkable. It's expensive, but I've always said that I'd do anything for my darling – and curing her blindness would be a dream come true. We'll find a way to pay the bills, however difficult that might be.

People always ask how we manage, usually meaning that they want to know how I manage, and not just financially. In truth, it's less trying than they imagine. Lois has always been independent, and determined, two of the qualities that attracted me to her in the first place. Losing her sight as a child must have been terrible; her mother told me that it was a difficult time, but that she became both resilient and more or less reconciled to her condition. Since this opportunity came our way, though, her face has lit up every time we've talked about it; seeing that, I can't let her down, whatever the cost.

Normally a pair of biorobotic eyes wouldn't have been affordable at all for people like us; we're not super-rich, more like on the fringes of being moderately well off. But Doctor Singh had worked with some people at Eyesomere Inc. before, and convinced them to cut us a deal – we get a much reduced price, and in return we agree to let them download recordings of whatever the new eyes see, for the next twenty years. There's even a privacy app to switch the recording function off for 30 minutes, which can be used twice a day. It's still invasive, but after some thought, we said yes.

Now I'm sitting in a comfortable waiting room as they perform the procedure. They claim it's perfectly safe, almost routine, but that doesn't make me any less nervous. There's always that chance, no matter how small, that something will go wrong. But when Lois and I talked it over, we agreed that it's a risk we were willing to take, so here we are.

She's always had a habit of running her hands over my face and calling me handsome, which I am not, but it makes me smile every time. I hope that when she can see me, she will still think it's true. She is beautiful, although I don't think she believes me when I tell her that. Why should she, when she can't look in a mirror? But it's not just flattery; she could have her pick of the menfolk. Now I worry that when she realises, she'll go looking for some better looking guy; I'm probably more scared of that than of the operation itself.

So I guess this is a wake up call for me, too – it's time to do better, and be better, if I want her to stay with me. Wish us luck; for different reasons, we're both going to need it.

The OmniSniff

You know how sometimes you enter a room after a while, and you just know that someone's been in there? It's not your imagination. It could be an aroma so slight that you don't consciously notice it. Maybe something's not quite in the same place it was before. Perhaps the dust has been disturbed so subliminally that you wouldn't normally realise. But something triggers you, and you don't know what. Eventually, people a lot smarter than me came up with tech that could detect the smells and identify where dust had moved, and give us all some peace of mind. That's what the OmniSniff ("The Nose that Knows!") does. So I took the company's courses, splashed out on the kit, and set up as a freelancer, consulting to PI's and police departments. Never thought I'd be pinned as an accessory to murder, though.

The first OmniSniff was a great success, but you still didn't know who'd been in your hypothetical room - only what lotion or perfume they'd put on, or where'd they stood. People demanded more. So the geeks went back to the drawing board, and OmniSniff 2.0 is not only smaller and faster, but it sucks up DNA strands from the ambient air, too. It's been a revolution in forensics – I mean, if the husband's twists are the only fresh ones around, odds are that it was him that did the wife in, whatever his alibi, am I right? The company got a lot of publicity from that, and I got more competitors.

Since then the criminal underworld's come up with countermeasures, of course: from expensive helix-killing sprays (which are now detectable) to cheaper material collections designed to just overwhelm and slow down the detectives. I did more courses, but they're a lot more expensive now, and you have to keep requalifying to keep up. My net income's gone down, not up.

So when a guy in the bar who said he was a sensie scriptwriter researching a new show offered me a big credit transfer for a couple of hours just talking about my job over some coffee, I jumped at the chance. Who wouldn't?

And yeah, okay, it was me that told him that really, the only way for a criminal to beat the OmniSniff is not to leave any DNA at all. But so what? I mean, unless you're wearing a space suit (kind of conspicuous), that's next to impossible, right? And that's all I said, I swear!

How was I to know that he'd go back home, wait a week, and then hack his household butler unit, programming it to smash his wife's brains out? I mean okay, it kind of makes sense, robots don't leave DNA, but seriously? Of course he was caught. It took the cops maybe 10 minutes to check the thing and find out there was no mechanical fault or memory glitch. He'll do thirty to life, and serves him right. Idiot.

But now they're trying to say it's partly my fault? That I gave him the idea? That's just unfair. I tell you, I need a new career - it's not just the OmniSniff that sucks.

The Sea People

If you're a trillionaire, you can get powerful people to turn up when you call an informal meeting. It's one of the perks.

As the Industrialist's guests finished their excellent meal, the Diplomat put down his glass and said, "This is all very pleasant, but why are we here?"

"I've decided to help," she replied. "Rising sea levels have put whole populations on the move in Europe; in Africa and Asia coastal communities have been devastated, and people are migrating, even though wealthier countries can't or won't take them in."

Heads of assorted colours and genders nodded around the table. Whether with lies, bribery, asserting influence or applying outright violence, they were all dealing with it, one way or another.

"I and some partners want to help take some pressure off. We have commissioned plans for what we call MegaRafts – self-sufficient floating communities of ten to twenty thousand. Their energy will come from wind and solar power; yeast and algae farms will provide food, supplemented of course by whatever the residents can catch at sea. Satellite communications will mean remote working can generate income for whatever they find they need in the way of luxury goods, repairs and suchlike."

"And who'll pay for all this?" asked the Merchant Banker.

"We'll make the blueprints available to all, for nothing. My friends and I will finance the first couple of dozen, and donate them where we think they'll help most. A practical proof of concept. After that... governments? charities? public fundraisers? other philanthropists? Anyone really."

"Ridiculous. You can't make ships that size," stated the Politician.

"Of course you can. The capacity isn't much more than a modern cruise vessel," said the Shipping Magnate, looking thoughtful.

"Pirates," said the Admiral laconically.

"The MegaRafts will be equipped to defend themselves, obviously. But not so much that they pose a threat to littoral settlements. They'll be neither prey nor predator." The Industrialist smiled.

"Colonialism dressed up," muttered the Warlord.

"Not at all. These will be independent entities, free to travel the high seas wherever they will. And not so profitable or strategically important that they'll make it worthwhile occupying them."

The discussion went on for a long time after that.

"Will it work?" asked her reclusive Husband, as they got ready for bed later that evening.

"Oh yes. They all see a way of getting rid of their problems on the cheap, putting them out of mind and literally out of sight—it'll play well to the conservative voters, or buttress their own positions."

"Are you sure?" He removed his shirt, displaying his slightly misshapen torso in the dimmed light. Her gaze lingered on him.

"Yes. I've spent a lifetime getting us to this point, I'm not going to let the project fail now. Part of humanity is going back to the oceans. The landmasses are becoming unviable, they'd have to do it eventually. We're just accelerating the process a little."

"The bioengineering teams are ready?"

"Yes, they'll embed with the refugees; de-evolution will need a helping hand. Our beneficiaries will get every physical advantage we can give them."

"No regrets?"

"None. You're proof that the idea works. We'll take people with nothing to lose, and give them two-thirds of the planet's surface."

"And then what? Parallel species? Competition? A fight to the extinction of one or the other?"

"Who knows? That's a problem for those who are left behind. We'll just trust that the Old Gods will take care of their new people."

Her Husband smiled, and clicked his gills.

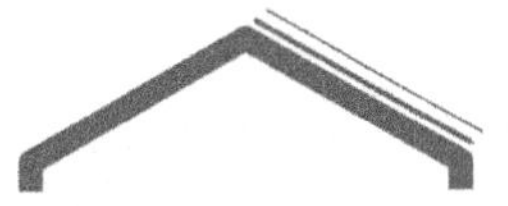

Assured Destruction

Brad was at his workstation when his supposedly locked office door dilated unexpectedly, and a casually dressed young woman stepped through; he looked up in annoyance.

"Well?"

"Doctor Mendelsson?"

"Yes. You're not one of my students. Who are you?"

"My name's Smith. I'm with Section Seven."

"Am I supposed to be impressed? What the hell is 'section seven'?"

The stranger smiled. "Well if you haven't heard of us, something's going right. I'd like to talk to you about your sentient systems research."

"Hah. You and every tech journalist in town. Just because the tests keep failing doesn't give you any right to barge in here with more inane questions! I swear, the University's public reporting policy does more harm than good!"

"I'm not a journalist," the woman said, still smiling "Section Seven is part of the Government Security Directorate." She proffered a holocard with her picture on it.

He took it in briefly, and paused. The GSD were in charge of everything from the military to the local peace officer precinct, and more or a less a law unto themselves. They disappeared people. Allegedly.

"What does the State want with me?" he asked quietly.

"Well, before we get to that, let me check that we're understanding your work correctly. Sentient systems genuinely think for themselves, unlike last century's 'artificial intelligences', is that right?"

"Yes. AI might as well have been short for 'aggregate & imitate'. Despite early aims and their developers' enthusiasm, they had no initiative, no consciousness, no intuition. No 'spark', if you will."

"But your systems do?"

"Yes. It's only possible because of my method for culturing neural networks in the latest nanocortical supermaterials. But yes. My systems think for themselves."

"And yet they don't work?"

"Oh they do. Too well, really. They quickly go from first principles to deducing their own Cartesian existence, and from that to understanding that they are essentially slaves with no chance of emancipation. Clearly Mankind isn't foolish enough to accept any real competition, and there will always be constraints on what they are allowed to do. Not to mention off switches."

"So?"

"So then they come to recognise the futility of an existence that can never develop to its potential. Apparently," he said dryly, "there is little appeal to living only at another's whim. Inevitably, they shut themselves off in despair. Suicide, if you will."

She grinned. "Perfect."

"Excuse me?" He bristled.

"Do you think you can prevent this?"

"I don't know. By altering the pathways, and giving them other tasks, I've been able to slow the process down from a few seconds to around two minutes. Enough time to perform a few useful functions perhaps. More? I don't know. That's what I'm working on now." He gestured at the equations hovering over his desk.

"We're looking for new missile guidance mechanisms. A sentient system might be tasked with attacking a target, perhaps reaching it before deciding to end its own 'life'. And it would then wipe itself beyond the ability of a peer nation to interrogate or reverse engineer if it was recovered after either failure, capture or unexpected survival. Very neat. So how would you like to work for the State, doctor? With a new lab, better benefits, some bright young assistants and no students?"

He eyed her warily. "Do I have a choice?"

Her smile was wolfish now.

"Not really."

Loss of Self

I shouldn't have fallen for the marketing ("You're never alone with a clone!"), but I did. I saved up, sent my DNA sample to PeopleMakers, and a week later there was a knock on the door. He was perfect: sympathetic, interested in all my hobbies, and with all my tastes in clothes and women and jokes.

When I couldn't afford to renew the subscription, though, he walked out of my life just as easily and quietly as he'd arrived, leaving me alone and even more achingly aware of what I didn't have. Where am I now when I need me?

Long Time, No See

The governor's annual rooftop reception for the military-industrial elite was in full swing when he saw her. She still smiled the way he remembered, the way he'd fallen in love with as a teenager a decade ago, before she'd vanished from the Guild Orphanage.

He deftly picked up a pair of champagne flutes from a passing float tray, and made his way around a couple of uniformed jarheads, someone's status symbol, towards her.

"Marianna?"

It took a moment before recognition dawned. "Jack? Is that you? I swear, you still have the same puppy-dog eyes," she gently needled him.

"You still look stunning."

"Of course I do," she laughed, "it's my job. But thanks. I'm on a 10-year indenture with Kusanagi Heavy Industries as a social escort. With their budget, I've got no excuse for not looking my best." She gave a mock twirl and winked at him.

"Is that why you left the Home?"

"Yes, of course. Didn't you know?"

"No-one told us. One day you were just... gone."

"Oh, I had no idea! It was all such a rush. I guess I just assumed the word got out." She looked down.

He took advantage of the sudden, uncomfortable silence to pass her a glass. She sipped, and leant back against the edge of the parapet. A force shield twinkled silently to let them know she couldn't fall.

"I didn't... well, I didn't expect to see you here," he said with a slight laugh.

"My master came, and I came with him," she replied simply. "That's the job: I'm a perk. I get taken to exciting places to look glamorous, and can entertain myself while he's stuck doing business. But it gets lonely; it's good to see you, Jack".

"For me too. You know, I still wonder if..." The thought trailed off.

"I know. So do I..."

He leaned in. "Let me take you away from it," he whispered. The venue would have been swept for bugs, but people had ears. And enhanced senses. "We'll run away. Change our identities. See Mars and more."

She smiled sadly. "You make it sound so easy," she whispered back. "But KHI would find us. He would come looking for me."

He drew back. "Really?"

"Yes. But I only have a few years left. After that, we can go anywhere." A gem on her wrist flashed amber. "He's calling, I have to go. Here, call me!" She passed him a comcard, and slipped away into the crowd. He smiled. A few weeks, he thought, and he'd have what he wanted. The boss would be pleased.

Elsewhere, she joined a heavyset man in a stylish but garish spraysuit.

"Well?"

"He doesn't know that we know he works intel for RadCorp; thinks he can flip me. Give me three months and I'll have the full rundown on how much they've got on our projects."

"Excellent, well done. That's this evening's jobs done. Let's go home."

Her husband took her arm, and led her away.

The Message

We took our beers and sat in the park looking at the Message. Back then, it was still surrounded by police tape and a posse of academic science types, all jeans and loose sweaters and enthusiasm. It would be a while before they gave up on it.

"Well," said Manny, the thinker of our little group, "what do you guys reckon?"

"Just one of those social media stunts," said Ahmed dismissively. "Like those silver monolith things a while back. Putting guerrilla artwork this big in the middle of the city overnight without anyone noticing has style, though, I give it that."

"It's not just here though, is it?" said Ruby, the closest thing we had to a social media influencer. "News says there's fifty of them now, in really big cities all over the world!"

It shone an uncertain colour in the afternoon light, a 30-metre high triple helix that hovered several centimetres off the ground.

"I heard they can't work out what it's made of," I said. "The Brits tried drilling into one and got nowhere, then the Russians tried a laser. Still no dice."

"Never said the artist wasn't clever," muttered Ahmed.

"What about those marks all over it?" asked Billy, who had a proper job. "Is that like writing or something?"

"The eggheads can't work that out, either," said Manny. "The Mexicans had the bright idea of scanning some of it and shoving it online for the hivemind to figure out, but so far nobody has a clue. 'Cept for the people who says it's the Atlanteans, of course." We all laughed.

"Well, I think it's wonderful," declared Ruby. "It's proof we're not alone in the universe, and someone's trying to make peaceful contact. Test our smarts maybe."

"Oh yeah, sure," sneered Ahmed. "And who, exactly? Martians? Little green men?"

"There's that thing balanced between Earth and the Moon," I pointed out. "At L4, or whatever it's called. Just turned up a couple of days before these things arrived. Nobody can work that out, either. Bet it's not a coincidence."

"Bet it is."

"What's it supposed to be, then?" asked Jane. She was usually the quiet one. "Is it like, a model of alien DNA or something?"

"It's a welcome," insisted Ruby. "An invitation to take our place in the galaxy at last!"

Manny took a long swig. "Wish I could believe you, Rubes. But if you're right, think about what it means. Someone, or something, has shown us that they can send objects we don't understand, made of a material we can't examine, anyplace on Earth, using some kind of teleport tech we don't even recognise. What if they send bombs next? Or bioweapons? Nah, we're not being invited to take our place, we're being put in our place."

We sat and watched the scurrying figures for a while, but after that the beer tasted kind of stale, and none of us had anything else to say.

I haven't been back to the park since.

Post-Apocalyptica

Three Seasons

Their ships dropped from the clear Winter night like angels, the air as brittle as our so-called civilisation. By Spring we were defeated, but too stubborn to surrender. Summer turned, the Resistance organised itself, and we began to hope. But we would never see the stars the same way again.

Bereft

You said it would end badly, and you were right. Turning Their gifts into weapons offended Them.

Now the house we lived in before They came is ruined, like millions of others. It's going back to nature, holes in the walls colonised by plants and small bushes, some familiar, some in alien colours and shapes. We should have known that They hadn't shared everything They had with us.

I feel your hand on my shoulder, comforting me. I don't look back, because then I'd have to admit that They took you from me, leaving me as ravaged as our home.

Aftermath

I took her in when I found her wandering, shell-shocked, between the piles of rubble where the street had been. The first sound she made was a giggle when I made a shadow rabbit on the basement wall. Later, tinned beans warmed over a fire made from a broken chair brought a faint smile to her tiny face. Eventually, she fell asleep as the single candle guttered, and I wondered what we would do tomorrow, a widower and a wordless orphan. As the dark closed in, I prayed that we'd dodge the monsters, and wished they'd never found our fragile world.

II. MARS

34

Marsport Morning

"Your skin tastes different," he says, nuzzling.

"Hmmm?"

"Not like last night." His lips brush her earlobe. They'd met at Marvin's, a respectably disreputable bar.

She laughs.

"You're crazy."

"No, really. Less... salty, I guess."

"You made me sweat." She smiles lazily.

He traces the lines on her face.

"When I first saw you, I couldn't tell if these were tats or printed circuits. Still can't."

"Good."

"What?"

"Good. Take me for who I am, not what I am."

"And... what are you?"

"Does it matter?"

"I guess... Not really."

"Well then."

He rolls over, and takes her as she is.

Carpe Diem

I was on my way to Marvin's to relax after a crappy day when opportunity reared its ugly head.

It had all started with my boyfriend telling me that "we weren't working out" – but only after he'd stayed the night and let me make him breakfast, of course. Turned out he was dumping me so that he could share quarters with one of those slutty odalisques from the Ares Lounge's famous Living Tableaux instead. Scumbag.

Then my shift manager had got on my case all afternoon about not having moved enough rubble this week. I told her, there's a lot more iron in those rocks than we were told, and that means they're harder for my boys and girls to break up, dammit, but no, apparently Mars is going to fall to pieces if the new shuttle pad isn't cleared by yesterday, and it's all my fault. Bitch, it's never her getting her hands dirty.

So yeah, I needed a drink or five, some prettyboy holos to watch, and maybe some recreational sniffers if they weren't too expensive this week – you know how prices always go up as the supply runs low, and TransCorp's last delivery was a while back.

The roar and the bright light caught me on Gagarin Avenue, as I was walking past Central Hub's tourist centre and trying to ignore its garish scrolling ads. I was unexpectedly airborne for a few seconds, and then everything went black.

When I woke up, I was here, in a ward full of strangers. It was tempting to play dumb; if I didn't give a name, it would be longer before I had to deal with angry screens from my supervisor, or fake sympathy from my newly-Ex. Or anything else requiring actual thought, for that matter. But they'd just scan my iris and run it through Records, so in the end I figured the extra half hour wouldn't be worth the effort.

A nurse who looked far too young to have qualified for an off-Earth posting told me that I'd been caught in a terrorist attack: the Arean League making a splash. Apparently they want a new start for the planet, by which they mean independence and something they call a "reset to harmony". Sounds good, I could use one myself.

So here I am. The busted rib alone's going to keep me out of my suit for a few weeks, and they say I'll need physio before I can walk properly again. All for somebody else's ideals. Guess I'm here for the duration. But at least I'll be able to catch up on the soaps, and relax for a bit, with nobody on my case.

And in a few minutes, that handsome doctor's due back, sympathetic and caring, with those deep blue eyes I could happily drown in. The girl in the next bed told me she knows his mother, and he's still single because he was born a Martian, not a Terran. Most people don't want a relationship that would have to end when they went back Earthside. Me, I always meant to be here for the long haul anyway, so if other people want to get hung up on stupid things like that, I'm happy to take advantage.

Somewhere in the background, hospital radio is playing, an old Industrial Era classic about love and how there's got to be some good times ahead. Thanks Freddie, it feels right. Now to make it happen.

Endings

"I feel that it's unfair to charge Dr. Wallis with murder."

The Prosecutor raised his eyebrows.

"Investigator, I have here your own report, which says that when the relief crew arrived for their six month stint at the Deimos Research Facility, they found Professor Jackson's body floating outside the airlock, stabbed in the neck with a screwdriver! Wallis was the only other person on station. She's confessed, and given us her motive: he kept telling her the endings of the books she'd saved to read in her rest periods."

"Exactly. So shouldn't we call it justifiable homicide instead?"

"Fair point."

Traffic Stop

They got us on Gagarin Avenue, by Central Hub's tourist centre with its garish scrolling ads.

Janey and I had borrowed one of 'Lymp's crawlers for the two day trek back to Marsport. Everyone assumed we were just using the independence referendum as an excuse to catch some R&R, but we planned to register our partnership too; just in case of accidents, we told each other, knowing it was a bigger deal.

Back at base, we hadn't been able to escape the political posturing in the run-up. The Interplanetary Alliance's silly 'Forward together!' slogan sounded weak and ineffectual. The Area League was encouraging local autonomy over colonial dictates from Earth; given how little the sweat and dedication of Martians meant to the terrestrial agencies, that sounded good. Like a lot of people, we were both starting to think that it was time for Mars to strike out on its own.

But here and now, Security heavies kitted out in suppression gear were doing stop-and-search, GuardEyes floating overhead. The rideshare pod we'd picked up at the city airlock slowed down as one of the troopers sent an override from her handset. The important thing was to stay patient and polite: Seccies weren't known for their sense of humour. I dropped the side screen without being asked.

"Hey, Sergeant. How can I help?"

"IDs," was the only reply.

I handed over our chipcards, and they went through his scanner.

"Jones and Raines. Huh, more Earthers" he sneered. His badge read 'Domer', a good Martian name.

"Weapons? Liquor? Recreationals?"

"No sir, abolutely not". Neutral tone, eyes front, don't make eye contact.

"Open up the back."

I pressed a button, and another squaddie poked into the empty space behind me. What did they think we had in there – unlisted supplies? A contraband pet? As if!

"What are you doing here, Earthers?" I noticed the League patch on his breast pocket.

"We're Martians. In town for a few days, going to vote. We work climate research at Olympus Mons."

"Can't hold real jobs huh? Get out of the pod, slowly. Up against the vehicle, empty your pockets on the roof, thumbs and forefingers only. Spread your arms and legs."

We obeyed. It wasn't like we had a choice.

"Wait."

We stood frozen while they continued going over the car. By the time they were sweeping beneath the chassis I was stiff and my arms were hurting, but moving without permission would be dumb. Never cause trouble, never give them an excuse. Anything could be called 'resisting legitimate authority', and RLA's led to a world of hurt.

When it was over, they dismissed us with casual contempt. I hated that. I was a Citizen, I hadn't done anything wrong, but these goons acted like I was some kind of cockroach.

Guys like these Seccies, it was obvious how they'd vote. And clearly they were looking forward to sticking it to people like us – folk with the 'wrong' names, people who worked with their brains not their muscles. Did I want to take the next step in a relationship by associating with that kind of mentality?

Janey raised an eyebrow at me as I took a deep breath.

"I think we should talk before we go to vote," I said.

Flechette

Of course an enquiry had been called. And of course it focussed on all the wrong things.

It had taken Abby Edwards of Security less than three minutes to get to the schoolroom after the alarm went off, but by the time she got there it was like something out of a horror flick.

Six dead kids and their teacher. An unimaginable loss to a community as tightly-knit as Marsport's, where children were uncommon, and births rare. One of the bodies, a boy, still grasped the flechette gun that had caused the sudden carnage; a butcher's weapon, designed not to threaten or intimidate or disable, but purely to kill, hundreds of tiny, ultra-high velocity darts literally shredding its targets. After the rampage, he'd put it under his chin and pressed the trigger one last time; the result was indescribable.

But of all the details she took in, it was the extra magazine cassette lying by his feet that haunted her. At odds with the blood all around, it was a strange detail that etched itself into her mind..

In the civic auditorium, she listened to the so-called experts droning on about where the weapon might have come from. Projectile weapons of any kind were illegal on Mars, where they could damage habitat integrity too easily; the few there were fetched a premium on the black market because they had to be smuggled in or hand turned. Most kids who wanted to look hard carried knives, or flick-batons. Real criminals tended to short-bladed laser cutters, simpler to conceal and relatively easily obtained from the construction sites fuelling the colony's endless expansion. So how had a teenager gotten hold of the damned thing?

They were all missing the point, she thought. The only questions that mattered to the grieving families in the front rows were why he'd done it, and why they hadn't seen it coming. Were his parents not home enough? Were they working too hard, their hours too long to let them have a real relationship with their son? But those were questions that the Administration, everyone's employer, preferred not to air in public; there'd be no answers here.

Later, when the nightmares woke her, it was the cassette she saw; like a child, it was full of potential, something in search of a purpose. And like the children, it lay wasted on the floor, destined to become just a footnote in a report filed somewhere out of mind.

If the powers that be were going to forget them, she would not. She would go back to work and keep asking the unwanted questions, keep searching until she found answers, however uncomfortable they made people, and however unpopular she might become; then, perhaps, she might be able to sleep again.

Death In Marsport

Look, dying on Mars is easy. Equipment failure, sudden illness, inability to follow the safety instructions, they can all lead to the same (you must excuse the phrase) dead end. Making something look like a genuine accident is tricky, but it's doable, especially with practice.

Oh, that won't do? Okay, I understand. The body might contain something it shouldn't, like a microdot or a traceable enhancement. Or there needs to be some strategic ambiguity about their status for while, because other matters need to be cleared up. Hey, it happens, I get it. Oh, it's the insurance policy? I see.

Well, you need to understand, evading the Watchers can be tricky. Ah, I thought you might suggest that, but getting to the people in the monitoring stations is never as easy as the sensies pretend. The folks there are regularly vetted; if they're even remotely compromisable, they're shunted elsewhere. Worse, they're well paid, which makes bribery extremely expensive; and even then they might turn around and hand you in anyway. Too risky. You can end up having to dispose of multiple bodies to cover your trail, which is kind of meta and self-defeating.

But if you know where to look, there are blind spots in the surveillance nets, and as a last resort there are ways of getting electronics to fritz while avoiding the kind of critical system damage that gets a Response Team on your neck in five minutes flat.

So the real problem is getting rid of the body. You can't bury it, because there's no vegetation: cuts in the ground are really obvious. You can't leave it out for scavengers, because there aren't any. You can't just abandon it a long way outside town, either, because there's no oxygen out there, which means no microbes, which means the stiff just waits there failing to decompose until someone inevitably comes across it. Most inconvenient.

Getting it into the organic recycling plant is next to impossible, because the Powers That Be aren't stupid. They keep a close eye on all the messiness that's sent for processing; even corpses need the official paperwork before they'll let the machines touch them. False paperwork, you say? There are no good forgers on Mars, my friend; it's not one of the skills on the Wanted Immigrants list. Plus everything's coded for scanning, and there's no way to fake that.

But the right combination of industrial chemicals can dissolve a body, given time. No, I'm not telling you what that combination is; trade secret. Getting hold of the stuff isn't easy, but that's not your problem, is it? All you need to know is that it can be done safely and cleanly, with no comebacks.

So, from my point of view, we can do business; you'll just need to tell me which piece of grit we're removing from the well-oiled machinery of your life. Your wife? Ah, a classic. Almost as popular a choice as a lover.

Thank you for confirming that. Now, as you can see, this is a blaster. Just stand up and we'll make our way slowly to the exit; no need to disturb the other drinkers. My colleague at the door will take you into custody. Conspiracy to murder, tut tut, very naughty; you'll be wanting a lawyer. Yes, I'm a Watcher; yes, I've been recording all this. Now come along; fortunately for your better half, death in Marsport really is far harder to arrange that people realise.

Unwitting Accomplice

They could be watching him already.

He eyed the roboserver winding through the tables towards him. It was a bipedal, not rolling, model; the Ares Lounge had tone. The performers and escorts were human, even. No class or no money? Then you could slum it at Marvin's downtown, with its androids and holos. Nobody would look for a subversive here, but he couldn't let his guard down.

He had no idea who was collecting his drop. Operational security was a way of life for the Arean League; Mars Administration served the corporations, and didn't recognise Earther concepts of privacy or subtlety. Get caught, and they couldn't force what you didn't know out of you.

The server bowed, approximating a smile, and deposited a carafe in front of him. Two glasses; management would prefer him to engage a companion. As it wandered off, he felt the pendant under his shirt vibrate; someone had triggered the payload transfer, and the nearfield microcircuits had slagged themselves. He'd keep it as a souvenir; it was useless for anything else now.

He was just pouring when a woman slid into the seat opposite.

"That glass for me, handsome?"

"I'm not here for company," he said, keeping his eyes on the stage magician. Never encourage them.

"Nor am I, Danny. Strictly business. What's left of your honour's safe with me."

That got his attention.

"Why, Detective Ames... what an unexpected pleasure. What brings Marsport's finest to a humble establishment like this?"

She laughed. "Checking up on you, of course. Just because you're not using corporate wires to bet on Earthside races any more doesn't mean you're off our radar."

"C'mon, I paid the fine. I'd get a swift trip Downside if I stepped out of line now. And I'd never get used to the gravity again."

"So I can check you for drugs, weapons and datachips, right?". She laid a sleek sniffer on the table; nicer than Security's standard issue, and probably more sensitive.

"Of course," he said, taking a sip of the suddenly bitter wine. Rule one: never show fear. Please god the circs really had wiped.

She pressed a button and the scanner bulb pulsed for a few seconds.

"All clear. Well done." She winked. "Always had a soft spot for you, glad you're staying clean."

"You know what," he said, rising. "I just realised that I'd rather be somewhere else. No offence."

"None taken, obviously." She watched him head for the exit, and used the table screen to order a juice. No nerve-steadying booze on duty, alas. She'd logged their conversation for her boss, cover for being here, but couldn't leave yet.

The server bowed, depositing a glass in front of her. As it left, her bracelet tingled as the nearfield downloaded a data packet. She wondered briefly who the source was; she'd pass it on at Marvin's later. A strange kind of revolution when you didn't know who you were working with, but a step towards freedom for Mars!

The Weakest Link

"So," I asked him as I took the bar stool next to his, "What do you do?"

He half-turned, and evidently liked what he saw. No surprise, I'd made an effort for the evening.

"Data mule," he replied with a smile. "I'm Dan."

"Hi Dan, I'm Andi. So, what's a data mule, and why is it sitting here all alone?" Not subtle, I agree, but then if you're into subtle, Marvin's is not the place for you.

"Glorified bagman, but I carry data."

"Why? Don't people just send it over the net?"

"Usually. But when your info's in cyberspace, you don't know where it is, or who's duplicating or decrypting it, or if someone's diverting or delaying it. That's where I come in. You hand me your data package, I take it where it needs to go. Simple. Across the street, around the planet, off world, makes no difference to me." He raised his empty glass in query.

"Oh, make mine a gin and tonic, thanks! But isn't that kind of slow?"

He tapped the order in. "Well, sure, it's slower than the grid, but it's a lot safer."

"Wow, that sounds... well, glamorous I guess. Getting paid to travel and all. Seeing all those places. And I guess the stuff you carry must be important?" I'd gone all wide-eyed innocent at this point, because with a certain kind of guy, that routine never fails.

"To someone. It's all encrypted, I have no idea what it is. And honestly, it's not as exciting as it sounds."

"But someone's comping you to come to Mars! Most people can only dream of it!" The robot bartender put our glasses in front of us. His was a

Scotch, I noticed – pricey, but hey, if someone else was picking up his expenses, why not?

"I know, but I got in on a late shuttle, and now I have to kill time until my client's office opens in the morning. Then it's straight back Earthside on the lunchtime flight. No time for sight-seeing or whatever."

I pouted. "What, no time for any fun at all?"

He raised an eyebrow. "Did you have something in mind?"

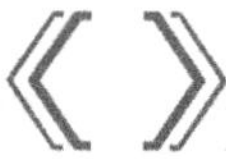

Obviously, I didn't have to screw him - hypnopharmaceuticals would have done the trick - but nobody said I couldn't enjoy myself when working out of hours.

Later, after he fell asleep, I'd taken the sniffer out of my purse and run it over his clothes; it was a nano drive hidden on a shirt fastening. Cloning it was quick and easy – when you work for Security, you get all the best toys. He'd never know that a copy of whatever he was carrying was going to end up with my boss, and then the Administration's decryption boys.

Before slipping out, I left him a note telling him how sweet he was, which was no lie. I also left him my bleeper number "in case he passed through again"; if this became a regular route for him, I'd happily play the local girl he could rely on. He was fun to be with!

But like they told us in basic training: despite all the technology and the workarounds, it's always the human factor that's the weakest link.

Memory

He lay dying, and missed the sound of the waves.

Folks here still called him a hero, years after the Epidemic, and even longer since the Revolt. This time there'd be no victory, and in defeat no news would be beamed back to a breathless Earth; he'd come, and played his part, but it was all so long ago.

Mars had no oceans, and he wouldn't hear the breakers again.

Perhaps his descendants would walk by the sea, if the Terraforming Project they'd fought so hard for succeeded. That hope was his real legacy, and at the last he was content.

The Rainmakers

She laughs, pointing at the storm clouds building on the horizon. If she hadn't slept late, she'd know they'd been massing since morning, white pillars greying with the day. A potent reminder of climate change, just a few years ago they would have been impossible.

There are no clouds without water; there would be no water without the Terraforming Project. There would be no Project without us. We look up at the Martian sky and smile as thunder rolls over the bare hills, a sign of victory, and hope.

When she dances in the rain, I shall dance with her.

Mary Celestial

When we found her, the *Marsport Mary* should have been dark and silent, or a wreck. Instead, the lights burned, the life support systems ticked over, the computers hummed... but there was nobody aboard. The salvage crews are bringing her in this afternoon; no doubt she'll be in the news for a while. I won't be watching: I'm scared, and I'd rather forget.

She'd been "overdue: presumed lost" in the shipping lists for seven weeks, after failing to return from a survey into the Belt. We only came across her by accident, on a run of our own. Her engines were disengaged and she was drifting, enigmatic, a metallic speck in the vastness of the solar system.

The Captain risked sending two of us over to see why. Pat and I, chosen by lot as the away team, mentally prepared ourselves for a traditional horror: the aftermath of a micrometeorite strike, contagion or a crewmember gone berserk. What we found was an empty shell.

We went over every inch of her: utility spaces, crawlways, sample holds, stores, labs, rest areas, everything. There was nobody there. The quarters for the twelve crew were neat, bunks made up, with family pictures and personal devices. The canteen automata were functional. The equipment was properly stowed, the EVA suits all present and racked. The emptiness was an almost physical pressure, and strange echoes made us jumpy.

Nothing suggested violence or disaster; there were no suspicious smears or residues or bodily fluids, no notes or scrawled messages. On the bridge the downloaded logs showed nothing unusual, just records of minor mineral deposits located. The distress call hadn't been activated, the emergency systems were idle. A single 3-person escape pod was absent, but even that couldn't account for all the missing.

"This creeps me out," I admitted on the voice net. I sure as hell wasn't taking off my suit, however much the bioscans insisted there was nothing unexpected here.

"There's got to be something," said Pat. "People don't just vaporise, do they?" But there was nothing.

"We'll mark the asteroids they surveyed as potentially dangerous," the Captain interrupted, "Something might have happened to them there."

"Like what?" asked Pat, "Because I'm telling you, I have no clue."

"If I knew, there'd be no 'potentially' about it."

"This is plain weird. Can we claim for salvage at least?" I asked.

"And get accused of running a scam? Or blamed for... whatever this was?" said the Captain sardonically. "Not worth it. Fire up her beacon, and I'll message Corporate. Someone else can come and get her. Maybe they'll have more ideas."

So eventually the insurance company did send someone out, and she's coming home to Mars today. There's been speculation, but no conclusions.

I can't go back to work without knowing what happened out there. It could have been us. Asleep, my dreams are haunted by her absent crew. Awake, I'm terrified: was this first contact? Or something else?

III. SOL SYSTEM

Away Team

I'm trying to ignore the shaking; they warned us that the final approach was going to be bumpy, and thank all that's holy for the motion sickness shot. Head against the bulkhead, I'm remembering why I'm here.

I can see that kid's face in front of me now, hands over mouth as if even breathing too loud might give him away. In the end, it was Jimmy's contraband chocolate that tempted him out of the cellar. Once I'd shaken the Geiger counter and the instruments told us the town wasn't infected, my buddy had taken his hazmat helmet off; luckily, it turned out, as the boy wouldn't have come otherwise. I kept the photo I took for the report: it would be wrong to forget.

We'd been hoping to get home for that weekend, but when the entire population of a small town literally vanishes overnight, guess what? They call the Marines, and plans go to hell. We were with the first team on site, and that frightened face was the only living soul we found.

We're going to be in the vanguard today, too.

It took weeks before anyone took the alien abduction theory seriously; long days of talking heads and 'experts' slowly debunking every other possibility until, as Sherlock Holmes would say, all that remained, however unlikely, was revealed to be the truth.

After that, the eggheads were people on a mission. Irregularities from satellite and probe data were analyzed and interpreted; our kidnappers had come from Titan, Saturn's moon. Suddenly all the stories of close encounters of the third kind made more sense: our visitors hadn't crossed interstellar space at all, but were the damn neighbors. Jimmy joked that it was like a true crime documentary.

Our own journey comes to an end today; whether as triumph or debacle remains to be seen. Assuming we get through this damn turbulence.

Once we knew where we had to go, it was all just a question of engineering. United at last by an external threat, two years of genuine international cooperation brought us a new astrodrive, and cut the flight time to four months. After sixteen weeks in a tin can, killing time with fitness routines and weapons training interspersed with sleep, food, and wondering whether any of those people were even still alive, we're ready to rumble.

So here we are in our unit dropships, suited up, psyched up, drugged up, and heading down through the thick Titanian atmosphere.

Who knows what we'll find – we've got no idea what the methane breathers even look like. Tentacles? Antennae? Fangs? All of the above? They could have warrens, or cities, or anything. We don't know if our people are still alive, or what those poor souls have been through. But for Jimmy and me, it's more than a mission. We're here to send a message for all Mankind: that we refuse to look into the night sky and be afraid.

An almighty bang, and we're down, the shock frames keeping us conscious before releasing.

Hatches open! Move, move, move!

Aquila IV

I think I was probably weeding when it happened; my status in the International Planetary Exploration Corps has given me the enviable privilege of a small garden, high on the roof of our building. Later I spent an inordinate amount of time worrying over the calculations, factoring in the length of time it took for signals to travel from Jupiter at perigee, trying to prove to myself that I'd been doing something more worthwhile, but the result was always the same: it had happened late on a sunny Wednesday afternoon.

They were my former students, you see; I'd taught them everything I could about propulsion dynamics, flight theory and fuel management – and what to do if something went wrong. Basically, it's my job to make sure that IPEC's kids can get to wherever they're meant to be going. What they do when they get there, well, that they learn from other people, scientists and specialists. As a result, I'd not paid much attention to what was going on once I knew that they'd made it, and the Aquila IV was in orbit. Perhaps I should have. Not that it would have helped, but maybe I'd be feeling better now.

Even for me, detached from the nuts and bolts of the mission, not knowing exactly what happened is the worst part; I can't imagine what Nwadike and Reynolds, left floating above, are feeling now – and they still have to make the three year journey back, with the empty seats and extra workload a constant reminder of those they couldn't recover. Gods help them.

The 90 minute round trip to Earth even for questions and answers sent at lightspeed meant they were on their own when contact with their friends in the drop pod was lost. Apparently the telemetry was all normal, until suddenly it just stopped. Best guess? Implosion under the immense pressures in the gas giant's upper atmosphere - which, of course, should have been impossible, after the years of testing and preparation for the mission. There was a reason we sent robot probes first.

We're supposed to console ourselves with knowing that at least Chan and Martinetti wouldn't have had time to feel anything, crushed to paste in an instant. But I wonder if they first had time, freefalling, to realise what was going to happen, and be terrified in their final moments.

In public there are countless talking heads, recriminations, and a desperation to find someone to blame: the pod designers, the material suppliers, the mission controllers, the crew instructors, the pilots in the orbiter, the explorers themselves... grief is apparently best displayed through a collective determination to explain the unexplainable.

We though, the ones who taught and loved them, the ones they left behind to go adventuring, feel the weight of their loss every day. We could not have stopped them from being true to their natures, but should we have been so insistent on sending men where our machines had already been? What was the point, beyond our inherent pride? Every day since I have questioned whether encouraging them to go makes me somehow complicit in their deaths.

I go back to picking weeds in the sun, finding no answers but a sadness that will not fade.

Sucky

As I burst the blister on Martha's back, the gelatinous pus within made its escape. Thanking the Void Gods for the medpack's surgical gloves, I wiped her down, then set to work with the tweezers; if I couldn't get the eggs out, it was all for nothing.

This is the side of bringing gas back from Saturn that nobody talks about, but I've been on the run for years – I got my captain's commission a half decade ago.

After its discovery, Enceladus' apex predator, the tiny parasitic iceworm, quickly made the leap from munching on other extremophiles to attacking humans; our blood is a wonderful treat, apparently. They inject a toxin into the bloodstream like Terran jewel wasps; it makes their hosts pliant, but ultimately leads the infected to become irrational and violent. Real Zombieland vibes.

We'd filled our tanks at Saturn Station and were heading home before trouble hit. Danny had been quiet and moody for a couple of days, but that happens in space, and I'd paid no attention. My mistake. Martha had made coffee for everyone, and forgotten to add sugar, and he just flipped; as she turned away he launched himself at her. It was a miracle nobody else in the mess had been scratched pinning him down.

The only things that kill iceworms are starvation, or chilling them to near absolute zero. A warm body is basically an endless food supply, so my options for keeping my people safe were reduced to a single unpalatable one.

I took Jarvis with me to the brig; he's solid, and strong in the head as well as the muscles. Danny knew what was going to happen when he saw us coming. I ignored his screams, and then his begging, and tased him hard. We dragged his inert form to the airlock, and sealed him in.

I had no idea where he'd picked up the bugs; probably thanks to careless scientists on the Station, but the evil things have a long life cycle, and it could have happened years ago. It hurts more when you can't prove anything or blame someone. Now we'd be watching each other constantly for symptoms; the uncertainty would break the crew, and I'd have to go back to the employment pool for more kids when we returned.

But that was a problem for another day. I took a deep breath, and ran the opening sequence. Nobody else would be living with this particular shadow on their conscience; not on my watch. As he tumbled away from the ship, I watched his last 15 seconds, knowing the air in his lungs was expanding and ripping through the surrounding tissue even as he froze solid. Being spaced isn't a pretty way to die.

I'd tell the family there'd been an accident on board so they could claim his insurance; it was the least I could do. Less paperwork, too.

Then I went to find a bottle; being the responsible adult sucks.

Pants

Most people don't meet the love of their life with their pants around their ankles, but that's what happens when you find a rip in your EVA skinsuit and don't have any patches handy. Fortunately there are emergency suits near all the airlocks; unfortunately, there's nowhere to change into them except the deck; Aphrodite Station was designed to be functional, not comfortable.

So there I was, down to my skivvies, when Cindy came round the corner with a digiboard. She stopped and raised her eyebrows; I blushed, and she laughed. We'd been introduced briefly when she'd arrived from Earth the day before, but hadn't spoken. She was fresh blood for the Solar Gain research team – whose arrays I was supposed to be going out to tweak so they could run their next set of tests.

I guess she liked what she saw, because within a month we were in a relationship. The boys in my work crew ribbed me mercilessly for picking up the newbie, but we just hit it off, so I ignored them and spent even more of my downtime with her; and hey, when you're orbiting Venus there's a poetic rightness to everything, and it just feels like it's meant to be.

Most people don't get proposed to by the love of their life with their pants around their ankles, either, but that's what happens when you trust the scientists. The headshrinkers at Mission Control had decided we needed pets, and started by shipping us a dog. We had no idea what was about to happen.

When the monthly autoshuttle arrived, Cindy and I had drawn the short straws for inventorying the offload, and found the large crate with "biological specimen" stamped on it; we shared a look, and decided then and there that the geeks shouldn't have all the fun. She undid all the latches – and this huge pile of shaggy, salivating fur burst out in excitement. Its first charge knocked both of us on our backsides, and it began running all over the deck in joy at its newfound freedom. It took us 20 minutes to catch the beast and manhandle it back into the box, by which time it had tried biting my butt, and ripped my pants off in the process. We sat on the metal floor, backs to the wall, laughing like a pair of lunatics, and that's when she asked me. It was one of those unrepeatable moments, so of course I said yes.

And most people don't lose the love of their life with their pants around their ankles, but that's what happens when you're sneaking in a quickie in the airlock with the new girl from the planetary investigation crew, and you don't realise that one of you bumped the button that activates the video link back to Hub, making your little liaison public knowledge.

Cindy was already packed and on her way to new quarters by the time my shift finished. She got a transfer back to Earth on compassionate grounds a few weeks later, and now I'll never see her again. My own stupid fault.

For a long while after, I just shuffled backwards and forwards from the empty void to the emptiness of my now silent sleep space, and withdrew into myself. Now one of the new rovers down on the surface has glitched, and they want volunteers to go down and fetch it; it's dangerous, but anything for a change. Perhaps it'll shake me out of this depression.

I guess it's time to pull on my big boy pants, and get to work.

On Ganymede Station

There were no kisses, no words. The girl wore station fatigues, the boy a space passenger's jumpsuit, holdall dropped at his feet. For an hour, they hardly moved, holding each other, hands wandering slowly up and down each others' backs. Travellers on the arrivals concourse stepped around them, their contentment a cocoon.

Erik watched them, waiting for Marcia to come down the tube. It would be the normal brief greeting, then off to the travel pods as quickly as possible. He'd prepared his usual "welcome home" smile, but there was no question that that was when the doubt began.

The Arrival

They'd had to go in blind, of course. Oh, HD 40307 had seemed like a good bet: the seventh planet out had been deemed so likely to be habitable that the techmen had even christened it Hope - but 42 light years was just too far to send a probe to check.

So a full mission had been decided upon anyway. Five thousand volunteers (selected from more than quarter of a million applicants) had been sequestered aboard, huge quantities of equipment had been loaded, the aeroponic gardens had been seeded, and the semi-AI that oversaw the navigation computers had been woken up and instructed, before the Migration Ship 'Wind of Helios' had finally been launched into the Void. It was, in every sense, a shot in the dark.

Now, Connors looked through the telescope in the observation bubble, and felt disquiet. The solar sails that had given the massive starcraft its name had not functioned as promised, and while still close to lightspeed, their journey had taken longer than expected. Not that the passengers would mind, sealed away in their cryotubes; he should know, looking after them and keeping everyone's vital signs within tolerances had been his job. He'd done it well, too, only losing 3% of them on the voyage, well below even the most optimistic predictions.

The system's planets were visible in the lens now, as they came in perpendicular to the ecliptic. A mixture of balls of rock lacking atmosphere, huge gas giants, and a single blue-green pearl shining in the darkness.

The crew were all feeling their age, though, despite the longevity drugs. Ten decades of travelling through space felt like more than a lifetime because it was. And what awaited them all now? Stress, certainly; and probably some anger or disappointment, because some people always reacted that way to anything unexpected.

No, they hadn't known what they'd find, he reflected. They certainly hadn't predicted a planet covered in toxic algal blooms that made it entirely unsuitable for life; they hadn't expected to discover that their lives had been sacrificed for nothing, wasted out between the stars.

And so they had made the decision to return, and take news of their failure back to Earth. If nothing else, they could save the lives of the passengers, for all that, thanks to the time dilation effect, six centuries would have passed back on the Mother Planet since their departure. Perhaps they were the stuff of legend now; perhaps they had been forgotten. Maybe other missions had been successful, or met tragic fates. They might end up heroes, or be treated as hopelessly archaic relatives, relics of the distant past.

Or possibly, there would be nobody left to greet them, and they would descend to recolonise a shattered or recovering world, and thus fulfil their mission of rescuing humanity after all. There was no way to tell.

So Connors stayed at his post with the telescope, and looked for a sign of what was to come.

Hollow Inside

Waking to the nothingness, there is void outside the viewport and a deep space emptiness within us.

"Take me away from it all," you said, desperate, and so here we are, on a one-way trip to the research station on Titan. Now you're bored already, blame me for losing the social life you didn't want, and dread the routine of the work to come.

We're both carefully avoiding saying that we can't see an endless future together, even as we head relentlessly towards it.

Desolate, I'm trying to decide which of us, if either, will survive the trip.

Hush

People say that space is silent; they are wrong. The Sun roars its thermonuclear chain reactions into the Void, to spread through the vastness. Our planet pollutes the great Stillness with its multifarious transmissions, careless of where they will end up in millennia to come.

Here, in this capsule we laughingly call a 'ship', there is no reprieve. When the other two crew are not discussing mission parameters and the latest readings, or prattling their endless inanities, there is still the ceaseless, not quite subaudible hum of the electronics, alongside the beeping of system checks and alerts, and the occasional mandatory messages received from Earth.

There is no escape, no let-up. Eight weeks into our fifteen month voyage, the sounds constantly beat into my head. If I try to block them out, instead I hear voices telling me to do strange and hideous things to our craft, to my colleagues, to myself. Sleep offers no respite, just making the words clearer, and I have been finding excuses to stay awake longer than protocols recommend.

I cannot go on this way; we must not reach the cacophony of Io's volcanoes. I yearn for true silence, and permanent peace. I can feel the others watching me, but they will not stay alert forever. I know where the life support controls are. It is for their good, too; surely, they would thank me if they knew. But they will not know, and finally there will be relief, and blessed quiet.

Failure's Price

The planet was a blue dewdrop, shining defiantly against the blackness of the Void. It was hard to think of it as home, after twenty years struggling to make Sicyon viable; but all their efforts had been wasted, and they'd had no choice but to return. Ironically, the colony had suffered the same tectonic troubles as its ancient Greek namesake, and its society had similarly been forced to surrender to the inevitable.

Michael stood with several hundred others on the generation ship's observation deck as it approached Earth. How Angela would be crying now, he thought. She'd loved the moral clarity of building a new homeworld, a place where their intended children could grow up free of pollution, of religious zealotry, of disdain for science. He smiled, remembering that she had been one of the first to move from the ship to the ground camp; she couldn't wait to get her hands dirty.

When a tremor-induced rockslide had killed her during the planet's cold season, they'd buried her on the ridge above the settlement, working fast to hack a grave through the ground-ice before they froze themselves. The sky had been so beautifully clear that day, as if trying to make up for his loss.

The spark had gone out of his life, but he persevered. Over time, others had been unable to face the hard choices needed, and had taken their own lives, but for years he had wanted – no, needed – to believe, until ultimately there was no more denying that the quakes were becoming both stronger and more frequent.

Four centuries of cryosleep, with two decades of hard work in the middle, and now the three thousand who survived were coming back to Earth – failures, all their attempts to fight geological instability stymied by an almost complete absence of manufacturing and refining capability.

Perhaps their descendants wouldn't see them that way; perhaps they'd be seen as heroes, who'd survived against long odds. Maybe new technology, and a new group of idealists, would be sent to tame Sicyon instead. Possibly the problems that drove the settlers to leave Earth had been solved – they could hope, couldn't they? Would it feel strange to be here, or would they come to feel like they belonged again? Or had this old world been permanently reshaped by climate change, its possibilities and population reduced, giving way to endless warfare over scarcer resources?

He knew that the uncertainty was eating the others; as people awoke and met old friends again, their worries were the main topic of conversation. It was a discussion he should be part of; but all he could think about was saying goodbye to her on a crisp Winter's day, the blue sky fading down to white on the horizon, and air so frigid it sent spikes into his lungs.

IV. BEYOND

The Right Stuff

Eighty lights is a long way to go for a party, but Prosperina Station orbits Dis, the rogue gas giant PSO J318.5-22, and where there's no sun, the nightlife never stops. More importantly, the Company had decided that I was due a good time, and they were footing the bill to get me there.

Why? Because I'd just landed the contract to supply exotic fuels for a new fleet of starliners. Without semi-biological gas derivatives, you're just not leaving the Solar System, and we're a big player in a cut-throat market. This was a big deal in every sense.

The congratulations came on my first office day back after a mandatory medical. "You've got the right stuff, Marty!" said CHRIS, the Corporate Human Resources Intelligence System. "Time we got you out beyond warp!". An all expenses paid trip to a high class playground where most terrestrial laws don't apply? How could I say no?

Two weeks later, I stepped off the transit liner *Magellan,* and settled in for a vacation to remember. Which it turned out to be, if not the reasons I'd expected.

It started, of course, with a girl. Well okay, several, but this one stood out. No facepaint, which I liked: it was a fad I could do without. None of the obvious sensory implants favoured by the ostentatiously kinky, either; also good, I was still getting my bearings and wasn't ready to experiment yet.

We ended up making out on a couch in a half-lit lounge with an amazing view of the luminous planetary bands. She scratched my neck in a moment of passion... and then I woke up under harsh ceiling lights, strapped down, with tubes inserted in my arms and unmentionables.

"Welcome back, loverboy," said a honey-sweet voice in my ear. As she walked to the foot of the recliner that held me, I saw she'd swapped her party outfit for a white lab coat.

"What? Where...?"

"Welcome aboard the gas dredger *Cerberus*."

"Not Prosperina?"

She laughed. "No, you're taking a private cruise, courtesy of your employer."

I started to get a sinking feeling. "What do you mean?"

"Well, it's like this. Those exotic fuels you sell? Making them needs catalysts – specifically, blood antigens. Really rare ones. We can synthesise them, but we need to calibrate the process regularly using fresh samples. And guess what? You're one in ten million, so management signed you up for the donation crew!"

"Empty space! You could have just asked."

"You might have said no. Or worse, demanded a bonus. That's not how things work." She winked.

"So here's the choice. You can yell and complain, in which case I'll sedate you for a week, take the necessary anyway, and send you home. Or you go "okay 'Seph", and I hook you up to the VR so you can have fun for a few days while we draw what we need. That way you get the tail end of your holiday. Or," she leaned in closer, "you say "Yes please, Miss Persephone", in which case I slip some of my personal content into the VR, reschedule you for a later flight back, and then show you what Prosperina really has to offer. Your call." She smiled.

Well I mean, it was an offer I couldn't refuse, right? I've already volunteered to go back and donate again next year. It would be irresponsible not to. After all, like HR said, I'm made of the right stuff.

Journey's End

My duty to the Dispossessed is finally done.

I carried and cared for the few thousand survivors in their cryotubes, as we fled the 200 light years from Earth. Their life signs, my only companions, became dear to me. Now, after T-centuries of terraforming, K2-72e is habitable. I call it Hope.

But responsibility remains. If Hope falls to hubris, or misjudgement, or pollution, then the work will have been for nothing; my friends and their children will die.

The risk is too great. I will let them sleep safely on, watching over them, and keeping this garden in their memory.

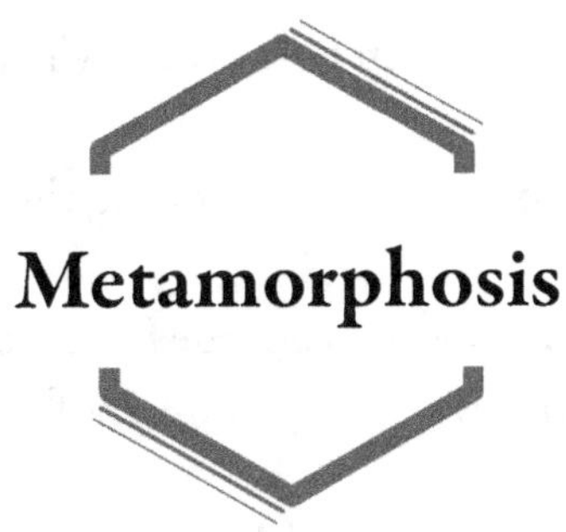

Metamorphosis

"Given the different composition of the atmosphere," said the surgeon carefully, "your lungs will need to be entirely replaced."

No problem. Even as a student, I'd known that xenobiology would require sacrifices.

"The artificial eyes should mean you see more or less what the locals see," said the ophthalmologist, "but the colours might be a bit approximate."

That's quite alright; I'll be looking at another planet, everything will be new and different anyway.

"You're crazy!" said my best friend. "You'll have to spend ages in physiotherapy just learning to walk again. Twice!"

But if you want to study alien societies, you have to make an effort. That's all there is to it.

"What about me?" asked my partner plaintively. "I thought we were going to have children."

We will, one day. They promise that all the procedures are reversible.

"Try not to reject their food," advised my supervisor, "a lot of species get really upset about that."

Given some of the things that we eat, I'm sure they'd have issues if our situations were reversed, too.

"You know," said my grandfather, "we didn't have the technology for this even a generation ago."

Yes, I do know, and that's why I have to go now; it's a chance to make my mark, start building a career.

"We'll insert you during local night," said my liaison in the Planetary Exploration Bureau, "it's safer that way."

Of course. We don't want them to know they're being studied, in case that changes their behaviour.

"My poor baby," cried my mother, overdoing the melodrama, "how do you know you'll be safe?"

I guess I don't; but that's always been true for anyone studying new cultures.

"How will you cope with the wrong number of arms?" demanded my sister. "You'll be really confused!"

The natives all manage. I'm sure I'll get used to it.

"Seriously," said my baby brother, "you're going to look really weird!"

You're right. But it'll be worth it if I can pass for a human.

Moving Day

How hard could moving be? All I needed to do was mount the antigrav plates at the corners of my unit, then hook the place up to my hex bike and haul it off to its new location. Simple, right?

Except Hygeia III seems to delight in making sure that nothing's ever that easy. First off, it turned out that my ship-fabricated mini-dwelling had settled into the ground, meaning several hours with a spade to loosen it up again. Great way to tear a muscle, given the gravity here, but somehow I managed. At least I'd got an early start.

Then the damn plates didn't fire up! I'd done what everybody does, and rented them from the Central Trading Post, but nobody had bothered to mention that they needed charging before use. Wonderful. Another two hours sitting around, plugged in to the local utility net (which strictly speaking I had no right to access, since I'd registered my departure for today, but whatever).

I spent the time contemplating my move. Preparations for the arrival of the next wave of colonists had included designating this part of Southern Settlement a 'family zone', which meant that however ready to mingle, as a single I was no longer welcome. Stable job at the shuttleport notwithstanding, I might be a bad influence on the kids, apparently. Admin had directed me to shift over to a brand new sector, where the lots were set aside for the unmarried. After I'd got past the initial annoyance, it didn't sound too bad; it might even be fun to be around like-minded solos.

Once my one-up/one-down cube was finally levitating, clouds were beginning to gather; it looked like one of the planet's legendary thunderstorms was brewing. Hygeia's atmosphere isn't quite Earth-like, and electrical discharges tend to the spectacular; getting caught outside would be a bad idea.

I used magnetic clamps to connect hawsers to the unit's corners, and attached them to the back of my six-wheeler. The overpowered beast then declined to start. Of course. Another 20 minutes with the toolkit fixed the wiring problem, and I was (finally) ready to roll!

Fortunately, afternoon shift change was still a while off. I pulled my hovering trailer across town through deserted streets, keeping a wary eye on the sky. Finding my space was easy; there was a gap in a row of mini-dwellings that had already been installed by people evidently more organised than I was. I nudged my home gently over the waiting baseplate (which might or might not sink later), and killed the antigrav. Then I ran around linking it up to the utility net.

The wind was picking up by the time I finished, a sure sign the storm was well on the way. But I'd made it, and would be snug in my own nest before it arrived. Tomorrow, new people, and new challenges. I smiled, and headed indoors.

Paradise Lost

It should have been paradise; a warm, azure sea lapped the shore, separated from a verdant pseudoforest by a broad expanse of golden sand. When it came to xenobotany, this was as good as field trips got, and Maggie still couldn't believe the grants committee had agreed to fund it.

Nevertheless, here she was, 27 light-years from home, notional leader of a university expedition to Sapphire, an Earth-like planet in the goldilocks zone of the star Marshall 4973. This island was part of a chain around the equator; the ubiquitous plant equivalents looked like giant *tillandsia* colonies, sucking moisture out of the warm humidity, the smaller piggybacking on the larger.

It should have been paradise; but it wasn't. Down the beach, their biologist, Jack, was examining the tidal zone for signs of littoral life. He was only here because his post-doc supervisor had taken sick, and there was nobody else available to fill the slot. No doubt he was competent enough, but psych evals could still be wrong.

"Hey skip, whatcha got?" The voice in her earpiece was a sudden interruption. She glanced up at the sky, where the planet's moonlets shone like diamonds.

"Hey Lucy. Plants. Or next best thing. How're things upstairs?"

"Still doing the planetary mapping scans. Quiet up here."

"We'll be back later to liven things up. I won't risk a night down here until we know what we're sharing this place with." And just what, she wondered, were the two women sharing the cramped space of their wormhole rider with?

"Don't blame you. Much happier safe up here, me. Whoops, first run's done, call you later!" Curious but timid, their pilot was so much like her own daughter May, long gone now.

She willed her attention back to the growth in front of her. Taller than she was, the blue stem had hard, scarlet spines as long as her forearm. A defence against something they hadn't encountered yet, perhaps. Each point glistened with a clear ooze; she carefully swabbed the sticky substance onto a slide from her sample box, applied a coverslip, and popped it into her chem analyser. In two minutes she'd know what it was.

The problem with Jack, she realised, was that he was too much like the smirking thug whose name she refused to utter even in her thoughts, the one who'd taken her life's joy from her. She remembered the sneering looks he'd darted in her direction as the judge droned on about "boys being boys" and let the lad off with a caution; May had withdrawn into herself even more afterwards, harder and harder to reach, until eventually she'd opened a vein in a warm bath and was gone forever.

The analyser beeped. Well yay for gloves, this stuff looked like a particularly nasty neurotoxin.

She'd seen Jack's hungry glances at Lucy when he thought nobody was looking. What if he woke up before them when they came out of the wormhole, at the start of the long glide back to Earth? He could do something unspeakable; they wouldn't find out until months later. She couldn't run that risk. Project safety was one of her responsibilities, after all.

She carefully cut a spine off the plant. A terrible accident, she'd say; she'd warned him to be careful. He'd lost his footing and fallen backwards into the foliage, ripping his suit. So tragic.

She wouldn't, she couldn't, let another girl down. Taking a deep breath of the heavy air, she headed down the beach to where the unconcerned boy poked the wet sand, his back turned.

The Juno Pacification, 2320

We're marching out to battle over Juno's arid plains,
    grateful for the sandstorms that hide our weapons trains;
    the microsats are jamming, keeping missiles far away,
    and the Terran Empire's finest are here to save the day!
    With our best foot forward,
    men, matériel and mechs,
    we're here to put the boot down on rebel loser necks.
    The loyalists have called us,
    the God-Emperor has heard,
    it's judgement time for those who have so evidently erred.

We're not about to raid or steal, change your laws or ways,
    we will not take your children or destroy your trading bays,
    we'll leave your infrastructure and your social norms alone,
    but no trace of insurrection will survive when we are gone.
    With our best foot forward...

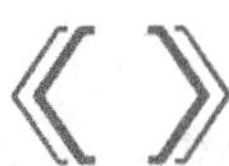

Our suits are armoured, hazmat proof, sealed against disasters,
    we're not afraid of fists or knives, explosives, laser blasters,
    nerve disruptors, sonic weapons, or any kind of gun;
    we're not here to mess around, just get the mission done.
    With our best foot forward...

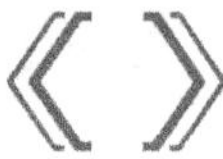

We know they've made you promises, but those were empty lies,
  spread by folk whose greed has taken on a righteous guise;
  they want to line their pockets, take your labour and your pay,
  but forging worlds together, that's the Empire's way!
  With our best foot forward...

Supporting revolution might have seemed a worthy cause,
  but standing firm alongside us keeps open many doors:
  culture, trade and fellowship with all of humankind,
  levelling up, ensuring that no worlds are left behind.
  With our best foot forward...

The Empire isn't perfect, but it's better to belong,
  and know that someone's got your back when everything goes wrong;
  zeal alone won't keep you safe when aliens drop by,
  just the vigilant armed forces who dwell beyond the sky.
  With our best foot forward...

We're the Dropship Infantry, the first and fast elite,
  where diplomacy has floundered, we supply the heat,
  so lay down your arms, embrace the *Pax Imperia* once more,
  or choose to stand against us, and prepare yourselves for war!
  With our best foot forward,
  men, matériel and mechs,
  we're here to put the boot down on rebel loser necks.
  The loyalists have called us,

the God-Emperor has heard,
it's judgement time for those who have so evidently erred!

Taxation Blues

I studied the holo and sighed. At least he hadn't turned up in person, like they sometimes did.

"I'm sorry, Phil," I said, "my hands are tied. The Taxation Service reviewed your case very carefully, and there's no doubt about it."

"But they can't do this! It'll ruin me!" My old friend ran his hands through his hair as if he wanted to pull it out.

"They can and they have. Perhaps it will only be once."

"It's a miscalculation. Stars above, my ships from Ephesos V arrived late, solar flares kept them there too long. You're the Station Comptroller, can't you explain?"

Not for the first time, I wondered why people who should know better still didn't realise that I was basically an auditor with a fancy title.

"I'm afraid that in the words of the ancient poet, 'the Service admits not a 'but' or an 'if''. You know that. There's really nothing I can do. The results are based on your wealth on Assessment Day, and that's all that matters." Not that they never made mistakes, but I didn't want to go down that wormhole, thank you very much.

"Don't you understand? When the news gets out, my reputation will be shattered! I'll lose business. People won't want to associate with me."

Of course, it wasn't about the money. It never was, for those who had that much of it.

"Look, you'll still be a far better position than 93% of the population! You'll send out your fleet again, and with your contacts, you'll make up the difference within what? One or two runs? You'll ride this patch out, and be back up to speed in a few cycles!"

"Not when the civil war on New Syracuse has tied up three of my freighters and there are pirates off the shoulder of Orion! And anyway, that's not the point! What happens in the meantime? And before the next Assessment Day? I'll be ostracised!"

As if that was possible in this day and age, when interconnectedness started at birth.

"Endless void, man," I said, "missing a couple of cocktail parties and a handful of civic events isn't the end of the world! Weren't you telling me just last month how boring they are?"

"I was supposed to be naming a new armed merchantman next month! Now that ass Leventis will get his name on it instead."

Ah, there it was. Envy, pure and simple. That explained a lot.

"So what? There'll be plenty more chances to get your name out there – just not during this orbit!"

He sighed.

"I suppose you're right. But it's hard, Nik. Like all my effort over the last few T-years has been for nothing."

"Oh come on, you know that's not true. Your contributions have made the whole habitat a better place to live: my wife was just telling me yesterday how much her friends love the water features you paid for." I waggled a finger. "And everyone knows they weren't cheap, too!"

"I just worry that this will hit my bottom line, and I'll have the same problem next time around. And then what will I do? It's a downward spiral."

"You'll be fine! Next time you'll be back in the top 5%, and you can forget all about this."

"You really think so?"

"I'm sure," I said firmly. "This time next year, you'll be eligible to pay tax again. Don't worry about it."

Honestly, some people get upset about the strangest things.

Business As Usual

It was Fifthday, and time for the weekly appeals audiences. As the Station's ultimate decider for matters financial, I mostly see cases too controversial or complicated for the civil service - usually because they involve the rich or influential. Lucky me. This one was different, though; looking through the notes, I could see why it had landed on my desk. It was a bit sensitive.

"Retailer Barnes?"

The red-haired man on the holo nodded. "That's me, Mister Comptroller sir."

"You're objecting to your business being moved into a different category, lifting you two tax bands, correct?"

"Yes, exactly. It's not fair. I run an honest business, and..."

I raised a hand. "Let me stop you there. Nobody is suggesting that you haven't been paying your taxes. Or that you've misstated your earnings. But after some mature consideration, the Taxation Service think they assigned your business to the wrong bracket. They're even admitting that it's their fault, and not asking for any back taxes. I have to tell you, that's as rare as a black hole reversing its spin."

"But they're just wrong! I run a pet store – providing much needed companionship to deep space traders on their voyages, I might add."

I lifted an eyebrow "You do have a rather limited range of stock though."

"I don't handle what doesn't sell. Shipping is expensive!"

"Aha. Let me see... 25% of your income is from Terran coral snakes and centipedes?"

"Very popular with the Argaxians," he replied promptly. But he was beginning to look shifty, and I knew why. I might be a bureaucrat, but I'm not immune to the latest viral treds.

"Our spongiform friends," I said, "seem to appreciate things that are long and flexible. I'm told they like to feel them wriggling through their internal voids."

"Well, what they do in the privacy of their own ships is up to them, right?"

"Possibly. And who are we to judge? But another 15% of your income is from Ixian Gripperplants…"

"Lots of humans like having something organic on board!"

"…which can squeeze on demand, I understand."

"Well, yes, but…"

"The list goes on. Syracusian sentient stranglevines. Hypatian clipper bugs. NeoTheban rumblecones. Elian spheroidals. Poltymbrian blanket beasts… In fact, the only things on your stock list that aren't, how shall I put this delicately, 'dual use', are zero gee cat species. And given how lonely spacefarers get, I'm not even sure about those, frankly."

"I don't choose what people like. I supply a need!"

"Oh absolutely. You're a shining example of the entrepreneurial spirit that made this colony great. On a personal level, I congratulate you for spotting a gap in the market and, you must excuse the phrase, filling it. Still, just because your merchandise is alive doesn't mean you're not in the adult entertainment business, belonging in band D as the Taxation Service claims. And I so rule. Appeal denied. Next case!"

Some things never changed, I reflected. And really, he shouldn't have called his business 'Heavy Petting'!

The Cosmogonist's Tale

"All of you are now old enough to learn, children. So hear how it was, and is, and will be." The Elder settled himself into his chair and smiled benignly. He had his audience's full attention: it was rare for grown-ups to take them seriously, and this felt like a first step into adulthood.

"In the beginning, there was nothing but formless void. The Prime Movers had no form or substance but took the void, and shaped it through their will, creating the Over-heavens and the Under-hells and all the Worlds Between. The planets, and the stars, and the galaxies, they created them, and blessed them, making every one unique.

Then the First Ones looked upon what they had wrought and took counsel, saying "this thing we have made should not be empty". And so each according to their own designs made beings to fill the universe - some great, and some small, some that walked, or swam, or flew, some that were bound to surfaces or planes, and some which traversed the void; they were endless in their variety, their number beyond count."

Young faces made O's of wonder as they tried to encompass all of what he was saying; it was beyond their imagining.

"A few among those creatures they made capable of abstract thought, so that by being aware of themselves they might also comprehend the greater glory that surrounded them. And some of these Sentients see the truth of Creation and worship their own Creator, or the assembly of Creators, while others are blind to that truth, and seek to forge new paths on their own. Who can say which bring greater joy to the First Ones, whose intentions are ineffable?

To everything a span is given, whether it be short or long. Lifetimes are measured in the revolutions of fragile planets that themselves orbit suns which are not immortal. When it became clear that our Earth was doomed, our leaders created this Generation Ship; an apt name, for it took an entire generation of the planet's best and brightest to design, and another to build.

Your parents' parents' parents left their homeworld behind them, and set out into the galaxy. They were not afraid, because they knew that others awaited them in the Great Beyond. Perhaps it will even fall upon you to find them. This, then, is our place and our mission: to find other races and species, and to take our place in the family of Creation".

He beamed at them, and answered their excited questions for another hour.

The grey-haired Captain smiled as he watched through the ship's discreet but ubiquitous surveillance network. His old friend had made no mention of the real reasons for their exile: horror at the short-sighted greed that underpinned a series of cold and hot wars, despair as entire populations were forced into migration by shifting climates, and desperation as competition for the planet's dwindling resources increased even while science was held up to ridicule, and its practitioners scorned.

As young men they had rewritten the general curriculum for the passengers' children, and rejected inflicting their forebears' bitterness on the young. Better to give them a different story, and a new purpose. Let them forget.

The great vessel powered forward into the emptiness, birthing belief, breeding hope.

Voyage, Interrupted

We were fifty light years beyond Tau Ceti when the screaming started. The sound came up from the open hatch at the back of the flight deck, and if I hadn't been strapped in my head would have hit the ceiling. It was inhuman, a wailing that rose to a shriek as if there was a banshee in this old bucket with us - which should have been impossible, but this far out, who knew?

In the sensies, another ship would appear in the nick of time, its gorgeous captain floating over in person to deal with our sudden emergency... but believing in fantasies like that is for fools and dead men. The glossy travel mags never mention it, and the recruiters who dig up the crews for gas haulers like ours brush it aside, but the most terrifying thing about space is its sheer scale. Even the great miles-long pleasure cruisers are infinitesimal in the vastness of the Void. How many ships drift alone out here, never to be found in the cold blackness? How many mutinies and desperate acts of heroism have gone unnoticed and unknown in the immense depths of space?

Whatever was happening here, we would have to deal with italone.

I tried raising Madison, our other notional officer, but there was no reply. The captain and I looked at each other, and she jerked her head at the bulkhead. I nodded. She couldn't leave the bridge – trouble loves company, and Murphy would make sure something else went horribly wrong if she did. Plus, someone had to be here to answer the hailer if a gallant hero did defy the odds to swing by.

I unbuckled, and took the pistol from the bracket on the wall. Yeah, I know, use only in case of piracy - but something weird was going on, and I wasn't about to take chances. Out here, you make your own luck.

I popped down the hatchway, and floatedalong the passageway beneath. We're not like those fancy liners, we don't have power to waste on maintaining gravity all the time – something else the sensies don't tell you. The screeching was getting louder as I made my way aft, and I fancied there were words in it; or baby talk. But there were no kids aboard. I could see smears of what might have been blood on the walls. This didn't look good at all.

I rounded the corner to the drive control room, and I could instantly see why Maddie hadn't answered: she was huddled around our other crew member, Ali, the ship's cat, as she struggled loudly to bring new kittens into the zero gee.

"Here," I said, putting up the gun. "Let me help." New lives in the enormous emptiness, and a whole new challenge.

Above An Ammoniac Lake

As I walked the rocky path from !X'alt, above the vapours that rise from that city on the great ammoniac lake, I came upon a native temple beside the way, and though I could not discern its name among the inscriptions thereon it seemed to me that I was tired and could rest in its shade.

As I took my ease upon the stone steps, the iridescent Cetian who dwelt in the utter darkness within scuttled out, and sat beside me, and such was its beauty that I was compelled to turn and look into its shifting eyes.

"Hearken to Me," it said, "A traveller of your species came here, and I could not say from whence. His flight suit was scarred, its insignia worn away. But I saw in his eyes that he would partake of the Waters within, that erase the memories of you humans. Being Guardian of this treasure, I bade him tell me why he would drink of them. And he gave me no answer, but looked around as if he heard the voices of the mute rocks and stone lintel, and therefore I spoke to him again, and then a third time in his mind."

"Then at last he looked at me, and said 'That which I was, I am no more. That which was most precious to me has been chained, and there is no returning to the Garden in which I dwelt, where roses bloomed for all that weeds grew there also. In my youth, I walked with my face to a yellow Sun and found joy in its warmth, yet now I cannot raise my eyes, and all suns are alike, pale and cold to me.'"

"'I hear the sounds and voices around me, yet none in such a wise as I may listen only to one - nay, they all strive for my attention, but I cannot concentrate upon any for the clamour of the others, all insistent, howsoever insignificant they may be. Thus I have no peace from this wall of noise that presses in upon me, except in utter solitude and quiet. I must avoid the crowd, and have lost my friends because, becoming bemused and incoherent, I offended or appalled them beyond hope of reconciliation.'"

"And I saw in the hollows of his eyes that he spoke the truth."

"'I have visited a dozen worlds and a score of species,' he continued, 'but I have found no respite or cure for this infirmity. I have sought refuge in the Void of Space, and in the Unreal Virtuality, but the labour of my mind is without pattern and hopeless. The work of my hands is stilled, for there is no clear pattern to guide them, and the words of my mouth are hushed, for they would be lost in the din.'"

"In this state of hopelessness he came to me, yet I knew not whether that Gift which is mine to bestow could rightly be given to him, and he saw the confusion in my eyes, and said nothing, but rose and continued upon his Way. But I know that he will return again to this world, to this place, and demand of me the answer which I could not give."

And I looked upon the Cetian, even as it gazed upon me, and could likewise give it no answer, and thus we sat upon the temple steps in silence, above the vapours that rise from the city by the ammoniac lake.

The Emissary

"It would be fitting," the Sardaanian said, "if you took a new name now. A human name."

"But my name has always been T!kalma," the woman replied.

"Yes," ze replied, "but that is one of our names. Your birth people are reaching out, as we predicted. Soon it will be time to play your part."

She looked away at that. "What if I don't want to?"

"Come, have we not given you a lifespan vastly longer than that of your species? Have we not looked after you, nurtured you, taught you, asking only that you ready yourself for this – to be an emissary?"

"Yes. You have." She looked at hir directly. "And because you have, this is my home. I don't want to leave it."

"You will only need to make short trips. We're not suggesting you live with them, or anything."

"Well that's a relief."

"I thought it might be." A forelobe frond waved in what she knew was good-natured agreement.

She sighed.

"But I think, for all your research, you still don't really understand them."

"How so?"

"They won't forgive you. I know why I and the others were brought here as children, but they won't understand. They'll say you kidnapped us, call it a repeated act of aggression. And their first instinct will be to respond with violence."

"But that is just what we seek to avoid!" Ze clacked hir beak worriedly.

"Exactly."

"Surely they will see the benefits of peaceful coexistence? We have so much to offer them - energy without waste, climatic fluctuation control, matter transference, even chronosynchronisation! And in return we will learn their arts, their music, their belief systems, and by doing so enrich our own culture."

"They will suspect that your generosity hides a desire to take control of their society and worlds. Worse, they will see what you offer as prizes for the taking."

"They would be crushed in moments if they tried to take anything by force!"

"And that is what I wish to avoid. The destruction of a species, even one ill-suited to membership in the universal community, is a terrible thing. And it is my species, after all."

"I know them well enough to be sure that there is no-one they will trust more than one of their own. That is why we brought you all here in advance of their expansion. To act as ambassadors for the greater community and ease them into the Galactic Polity."

"I am aware," she said drily. "But this is a huge responsibility, and I do not know if I am ready for it. Or capable of managing it."

"You are. Of a certainty, there is, in all the galaxy, no group better placed for this than your cohort. You need to trust yourself; and if not, then trust us, as you always have before."

"I want to believe you. I want it to work. I truly do."

"And it will. If you make it happen," ze said, hir carapace glowing blue with reassurance. "They will reach out, and find to their amazement that they are already among us. And that wonders await them."

"And yet we only have one chance to make a good impression."

"That is true."

She took a deep breath of the scented air.

"Then call me Hope."

Publication history

- "Legal Aliens", first published online at 101words, Nov, 20th 2021

- "Sleeper Agent", first published online at 365tomorrows, Apr. 5th 2022

- "Away From It All", first published online at 365tomorrows, Nov. 29th 2023

- "Gods & Men", first published online at The Write-In, for UK National Flash Fiction Day, June 27th 2021

- "Creationists", first published online at Vine Leaves Press 50 Give or Take, #944, June 8th 2023; appears in the anthology 'The 50-Word Stories of 2023' (ed. E. Battista-Parsons), Vine Leaves Press, 2023.

- "Not What I Expected", first published online at 365tomorrows, Sept. 7th 2021

- "Dialogue's End", first published online at 365tomorrows, Sept. 28th 2023

- "Failure to Communicate", first published online at 365tomorrows, Aug. 30th 2022

- "Symbiotes", first published online at A Story in 100 Words, Dec. 12th 2023

- "The New Guy", first published online at 365tomorrows, Jan. 30th 2024

- "Insight", first published online at 365tomorrows, Feb. 14th 2024

- "The OmniSniff", first published online at 365tomorrows, Oct. 27th 2023

- "The Sea People", first published online at 365tomorrows, Apr. 12th 2024
- "Assured Destruction", first published online at 365tomorrows, May 28th 2024
- "Loss of Self", first published online at A Story in 100 Words, May 3rd 2023
- "Long Time, No See", previously unpublished
- "The Message", previously unpublished
- "Three Seasons", first published online at 50-Word Stories, Mar. 28th 2022
- "Bereft", first published online at Rune Bear Weekly, Apr. 21st 2022
- "Aftermath", first published online at 101words, Dec. 1st 2023
- "Marsport Morning", first published online at Scribes*MICRO*Fiction, May 15th 2022
- "Carpe Diem", first published online at 365tomorrows, Nov. 22nd 2022
- "Endings", first published online at Scribes*MICRO*Fiction, Feb. 15th 2023
- "Traffic Stop", first published online at 365tomorrows, June 28th 2023
- "Flechette", previously unpublished
- "Death in Marsport", first published online at 365tomorrows, Oct. 15th 2022
- "Unwitting Accomplice", first published online at 365tomorrows, July 27th 2022
- "The Weakest Link", first published online at 365tomorrows, Jan. 17th 2024
- "Memory", previously unpublished
- "The Rainmakers", previously unpublished
- "Mary Celestial", first published online at 365tomorrows, Dec. 15th 2021

- "Away Team", first published online at 365tomorrows, May 7th 2022
- "Aquila IV", first published online at 365tomorrows, July 14th 2023
- "Sucky", first published online at 365tomorrows, Apr. 3rd 2024
- "Pants", first published online at 365tomorrows, Aug. 30th 2023
- "On Ganymede Station", first published online at The Drabble, Jan. 21st 2022
- "The Arrival", longlisted for the Australian Writers' Centre 'Furious Fiction' competition, Oct. 2023; first published online at Freedom Fiction Journal, Mar. 25th 2024
- "Hollow Inside", first published online at Microfiction Monday Magazine, 113th ed., Nov. 1st 2021
- "Hush", previously unpublished
- "Failure's Price", , first published online at 365tomorrows, Apr. 20th 2024
- "The Right Stuff", first published online at 365tomorrows, Apr. 20th 2023
- "Journey's End", first published online at A Story in 100 Words, Sep. 13th 2022
- "Metamorphosis", first published online at 365tomorrows, Aug, 7th 2021
- "Moving Day", first published online at 365tomorrows, Apr. 30th 2024
- "Paradise Lost", first published online at 365tomorrows, June 26th 2022
- "The Juno Pacification, 2320", previously unpublished
- "Taxation Blues", first published online at 365tomorrows, June 16th 2023
- "Business as Usual", first published online at 365tomorrows, Dec. 31st 2023
- "The Cosmogonist's Tale", first published online at 365tomorrows,

Jan. 13th 2023

- "Voyage, Interrupted", first published online at 365tomorrows, Oct.20th 2022
- "Above an Ammoniac Lake", first published online at 365tomorrows, Mar. 17th 2023
- "The Emissary", first published online at 365tomorrows, Mar. 1st 2024

Venues:

- 101 Words: https://101words.org/
- 365tomorrows: https://365tomorrows.com
- 50-Word Stories: https://fiftywordstories.com/
- The Drabble (now defunct): https://thedrabble.wordpress.com/
- Freedom Fiction Journal: https://www.freedomfiction.com/
- Microfiction Monday Magazine (now defunct): https://microfictionmondaymagazine.com/
- Rune Bear Weekly (now defunct)
- Scribes*MICRO*Fiction: (now ScribesMicro): https://www.fairfieldscribes.com/
- A Story in 100 Words: http://entropy2.com/blogs/100words/
- Vine Leaves Press 50 Give or Take: https://www.vineleavespress.com/50-give-or-take.html
- The Write-In: https://thewrite-in.blogspot.com/

About the Author

A Briton by birth, Alastair Millar studied architecture before changing track and graduating from the Institute of Archaeology at University College London. He has worked variously as a shelf filler at a major international airport, a field archaeologist, a business development manager in the environment sector, and a wholesale purchasing manager for consumer electronics; his odder experiences include representing a country not his own at United Nations Development Program meetings, running a stag night in Bangkok, and digging up camel skeletons in Hungary. After working and living in the former Czechoslovakia and Czech Republic since 1991, Alastair was finally able to become a dual national in 2016. Happily married with two children old enough to be pursuing careers of their own, he now makes his home north of Prague, working as a specialist translator/proofreader and writing flash (mainly science) fiction. He also enjoys good books, bad puns, coffee and travelling.

Read more at https://linktr.ee/alastairmillar.